CHRYSANTHEMOM

SATISHCHANDRA MARUTRAO GAIKWAD

First Published in August 2021

ISBN: 978-93-5472-117-5

BLUEROSE PUBLISHERS

www.bluerosepublishers.com

info@bluerosepublishers.com

+91 8882 898 898

Cover Design:

Muskan Sachdeva

Typographic Design:

Tanya Raj Upadhyay

Distributed by: BlueRose, Amazon, Flipkart

Dedicated to

1)Tai
In my journey of life she is like standstill North
Star !

And 2) Surendra
Millions rays shining his notebook lines!

Preface

I was born in a village in Sahyadri mountain range. My mother's name was Shevanti (means Chrysanthemum in Marathi language) she used to take me to farmland on bank of Brook in childhood. There she would show me Green Bee Eater skillfully spinning in the air to catch insects, Minnows swimming in clear water and would make me listen to bleating lambs attentively. She induced in me love for poetry

These small instances in early childhood impacted my amorphous mind and molded it into sensitive receptor which continued to receive signals from the Nature's treasures like birds, flowers and so many others and turned them into fountain of emotions-joy or sorrow its colorful jets.

Whenever I see Chrysanthemum flower my hands are reflexly folded for Namaskar or when I read letters of word 'Chrysanthemum ' the U in it folds hands and becomes O and then I read the word as 'Chrysanthemom' remembering my 'Mom' Shevanti!

Chrysanthemum is universal flower connected to human civilization through centuries. In Japan it represents longevity and rejunivation. In Europe given for comfort in grief and bevereament. My 'Chrysanthemom ' I hope will give some comfort in days of Covid when humanity as a whole is in grief.

My special thanks to Varsha Ajaykumar, Hemant, Nikhil and Rajendra Lokhande for their assistance. But for their encouragement the Chrysanthemom would not have bloomed.

Satish Gaikwad May 12th 2021

Contents

1) Blooming Krishna-Kamal

Oh my Lord !
You made me small Ant
How can I see your Universe ?
Minute are my eyes
Vast boundless is the Universe !

And the God
Listened to the Ant's prayer
And opened petals of Krishna-Kamal
For the Ant to see the Universe

And said the Ant
"Colorful is the Universe
Honey sweet it is ! "

Satish Gaikwad November 25th 2020

(on watching a video by Ravindra Gaikwad
Blooming Krishna-Kamal and an Ant on it)

2) Heron

Peering his image
In undulating water-mirror
Stands still the Heron
No prey in sight
One jerk at neck
And darts the beak
A fish held high
A magic trick!
Displaying the trophy
Straightens the neck long
Thus got over the waiting long

Rumble in water
Instantly dies
And undulating mirror
For a moment cries !

3) Mangrove forest Lokhandwala

Abutting my backyard ground
Huge patch of Mangroves forest
Envied by Skyscrapers around
The home for creatures to live and rest.

Sweetly sing Cuckoo and Skylark
Like an arrow Kingfishers dart
In night mournfully foxes bark
And hoot white Owls in darkest part

On high tide days Backwaters rush
Carrying along with School of fish
To meet friends and lay eggs there
Crabs and Tortoises happily live where

An evening sets in scarlet sky
And over worked Herons skyward fly
The Moon comes smiling large and white
Showering Mangroves with silvery light

In Lokhandwala Cement Jungle
An Oasis that's 'Flora and Fauna's delight
Away from city's Chaotic Tangle
Languid forest bathes in Moonlight

4) Buddha Purnima

On bank of the lake, stands Gulmohar in Scarlet
attire ---
- Watching enthralled Swan peering at floating
image of the Moon on water.
As serene Moon smilingly cruises in sky
On Buddha Purnima Night.

Westerly breeze Jasmine fragrance wafts
And white Owl lands on Gulmohar soft
Carrying message from the 'Asia's Light '
Meditates the Wise Owl in silvery - Moonlight .

Peaceful Night, Peace everywhere
No hustle, no rustle, standstill Air
Pondering Owl and languid Swan
Veil of Tranquility slowly spreads on

"Who! Who! Who!" Hooted the wise bird
Resonated the sky and smiling Moon heard
Echoes in words "Me -- Man's peace "
"Me -- Universe's Soul " "Me -- Coexistence "

5) Ramu-Baba the Shepherd

In Sahyadri's Moutain Range
Lived Ramu the Shepherd .
Shouldered Crook and Turban on head
Story of Ramu have you ever heard?

In twitters of the birds
At Sunrise would wake up the Shepherd
And one glance at the sheep - herd
He would smile and say few words

And the flock of sheep would surround him
Many ewes, few lambs and two rams amongst
them!
"Baa! Baa!" All of them would say "Hi"!
In joy, as their loving Master was nearby!

In the flock of black sheep one Lamb, Snow white
Named 'Balu' by Ramu's daughter Prema
Stood apart like full Moon in dark clouded night!
Balu the Darling of Prema and her
Ramu-Baba .

Every Saturday weekly Shenoli-Bazar
Ramu would sell to Butcher one lamb

And purchase grocery and mutton so far
On that day it was turn of 'snow-white' lamb

"Baba!" "Don't sell 'Balu- my Darling '
Said sobbing Prema in grief yearning!
As Ramu carried the lamb to Butcher for sale
"Ba!Ba!" "Baba!" Cried the lamb pitiable!

In Butcher's Iron Clasp, stared the lamb in
Ramu's eyes, bleating "Ba! Ba!" he asked
And heard Ramu " Baba! Am I not your child?"
Shuddered the Shepherd speechless, and eyes open
wide!

Baba Ramu --- "Ba Ba" White Lamb
Bye Bye Ramu...... Bye Bye White Lamb!
Satish Gaikwad dated December 9th 2020

6) Story of Midnight

It's Midnight---
I am awake, eyes wide open,
My friend Owl on Gulmohar tree
Faithfully giving me company!

In Ocean of Darkness
The Owl is submerged in darkness
Nothing is seen of him but the Diamond Eyes
Penetrating the heart of darkness.

Quiet is the Owl
Ouiet am I.
Standstill Gulmohar
Standstill Air

Sly minute arm of the clock
Moves slowly but silently
And distant dog mournfully howls
Breaking the silence harshly.

Shuddered the Owl but for a moment
And cried shrill "Who! Who! Who!".
The hooting is answered by barking dog

In secret, mystical language they continued their dialogue!

Minute arm moved many hours
Night grew darker and darker.
And the wise bird whirled head in circle
Rotating the shining bright eyes like search light of the Light House!

Ocean of Darkness goes silent and still
And sleeps night dark with thousand secrets in heart buried!
Satish Gaikwad dated December 12th 2020

7) Master Dada the Headmaster

In Sahyadri Moutain Range
Lies one Shenoli-Village,
Sheltering few thousands lives
Likc bees on hives!

Illiterate farmers and men of all trades
With cattle and birds in nests they made,
Happily lived in Village with no electric light
In day Sunlight and starry or Moonlit nights!

'Master-Dada' the Headmaster in local school
Teacher by profession and farmer by choice,
Nurtured young students in the school
And crops in the fields,like Jowar and Rice!

On 'August 15th 1947' Master-Dada painted
The school wall, calibrating with brush
Announcement of India's Independence in his
fashion!
And addressed the students to be 'Light of
Newborn Nation'!

In midnight, in lantern dim light
He would narrate stories of Shivaji,Gandhi and
Ambedkar

To his neighbors illiterate
And take oath from them
'Every home will have one graduate or at least one
literate!'

Years passed by, and the Village
Proudly boasts of graduates inhouse;
Now there is Electricity light
But more shines 'Education the Bright'!

Satish Gaikwad dated December 11th 2020

8) Covid Warrior

The Doctor in his chamber tranquil
Reassuring his sneezing patient;
'Buddha's smile' on his face
No fear, No worry not even trace.

While invisible particle of Virus
Sneezed to set Cyclone
In humanity's 'Pacific Ocean'
To sink thousands of vessels
In violent waves of fear.

Few days later..........
The Doctor on ventilator
Struggling for breath
As frighteningly stared at him the Death!

The Warrior with forty years 'war-skill'
Who defeated the Death thousands of times
Was fighting the obnoxious 'invisible with hidden skill'
To lose the battle fought so well.

Death proved to be supreme over the 'Covid Warrior'
Body in shroud and poignant Air

In vain searches the hearse,ground for funeral
Refusal everywhere as 'Covid Corpse' was untouchable!

Combed every corner and nook
'No' everywhere and hateful look;
No place for 'Covid Warrior'
To Rest in Peace!

In Death learned the 'Warrior' the truth,
Along with creating facilities and space
For treating his Covid patients well;
For his Tomb, he should have provided some place!
Satish Gaikwad December 13th 2020

9) Scarborough in England

My daughter received me at station in
Scarborough ......
When in Roses,was smiling the Spring
Seagulls were flying in the clear sky
Like Angle on white wings!

Her home was on a hillock,
Moutain Range standing tall behind,
Lapping waters in a brook aside
And mewing Seagulls flying around!

City of Seagulls and Roses,
Roses here, seagulls there and joy everywhere!
Loving daughter and lapping water
Veil of mist dawn to dusk and Linnets twitter!

One church nearby its tower kissing the sky
And puzzled Sycamore staring in awe!
One day, one seagull's wing got entangled,
In windowsill of the church God knows how!

Fire brigade boys rescued the seagull,
With one wing broken, seagull woebegone!

Sky dream broken, flying hopes gone,
Tears in eyes and mewing in moan!

One seagull sits on my mind's bough,
Whenever I remember Scarborough !
Beautiful roses and lapping waters of Spring,
And in ears, Seagull's mewing,moaning rings!
Satish Gaikwad dated December 16th 2020

10) The Farmer

The farmer toiling in the field
Looked up to the burning Sun
And pleaded " Sun-God, please stop it"
"Thirsty and dried up is the Earth and helpless
me"

Smiled the Sun and said "I am heating for you the
'Ocean' to boiling point "
"For it to exhale vapours to form clouds umbrella
for you!"
And comes June ......

The Sun hides himself behind the clouds
Torrential rains poured down
The Earth quenched her thirst
With folded hands the farmer was to thank the
clouds first!

'Sprouting of plants ' news on Air
Flying birds sing songs of 'harvest fair'!
Satisfied farmers as granaries are full
Dance on 'Baishakhi' smiling Moon full !
Satish Gaikwad December 20th 2020

11) Godess Akaladevi of Shenoli

The Monsoon clouds flock
Over modest Sahyadri Range,
To pay respect to 'Godess Akaladevi'
Like woolly black sheep!

Showering over the Godess
They meltdown into water in Renaissance!
And springs out a rivulet,
From head of the Godess
Like the Ganga from Shiva's head!

Plunged in the valley the garrulous waterfall,
Quickly running the Brook with the
Godess's message to Shenoli-villager's call!
On the way, feeding the ponds and lake where
lotuses float,
And watering the plants as they sought!

In Shravan the month of August
Mountain and meadows wear green attire
While ornamental flowers decorate the
mountain's footland
As in colorful clothes dance ladies in ring
Merrily flying birds in the sky sing!

At break of dawn, scarlet Sun rises in sky,
From behind the Akaladevi Temple on the
mountain,
Salute the villagers with folded hands
As faith and love go hand in hand !

Satish Gaikwad December 19th 2020

12) The Lizard

In my backyard,
I often see one Lizard.
Neck straight with head held high,
And wide open, slit pod like eyes !

Pride in posture, pride in eyes
No trace of fright in eyes
But secrets of many years and some lies
Like 'Dinosaur is my forefather' and 'I don't lie' !

Nictating membrane moves like shutter
But for a moment and eyes tell story lie utter!
"Why should I bother who is nearby ?"
"May it be a tiger or an eagle in the sky!"
"On my feet I hold my ground and I don't lie"

Elbows akimbo he does sit-ups
Like a wrestler in gym ;
And scurrying, in worry he runs up
When closer I move to make friendship.

Oh! Dinosaur's great grandson,
To you what the evolution has done !

Savage in you is taken away in fact,
But the pride in self kept intact !

Satish Gaikwad December 23rd 2020

13) The Doctor

It's world of nocturnals
Mute white Owl on Gulmohar,
Barking dogs on street
And pondering Doctor in bed room!

Crescent Moon sailing in the sky
Night sips 'sweet-and-sour' wine in joy
World in slumber in sweet and sour dreams
And softly flows the near by water stream !

Doctor in deep thought
How to face the challenge Covid has brought?
Patients in ICU struggling for breath
Where is the sword to fight Covid with?

Through the window of his bedroom,
Gazing at the Owl, the Doctor pensive ;
Saw, 'like an arrow darted down the Owl,
Caught a rat in his claw and slew'
And in moment happily skywards flew!

Shuddered the night , tears in the eyes ,
Howling dogs loudly cry....and cry,

Sickle of the Moon hanging in the sky ,
And the stream of water continued to flow with a

grin wry !
Satish Gaikwad December 21st 2020

14) Rooster King

The Rooster- bright red comb on his head,
On breast, colorful feather armour like army head,
Tail like rainbows in clear sky,
And brightly shining stars in eyes !

Stands firm and looking at the sky,
Crowing loudly like triumph cry !
Hurriedly vanishes the frightened night,
And breaks dawn, happy and bright !

Scarlet paints the Sun, eastern sky,
Looking at the Sun, the King is crowing high,
Like blowing trumpet over winning of a battle,
And happily swings the red wattle !

Head held high skyward looking,
Proudly displays, the King his colorful wings,
Upwards sails the Sun smiling,
And for their King, the birds in sky happily sing !
Satish Gaikwad December 25th 2020

15) Melancholy

Life is interwoven web with sorrow and joy
Who has escaped sorrow in the web of life?
So why not Melancholy you enjoy !
Darker is the night brighter are stars !

World is in slumber, Melancholy you gaze at the
sky,
Twinkle the stars but woebegone you are ; why?
Night breeds morn then why do you mourn ?
Wash out your sorrows in tears in your eyes !

Bleeding heart will breed songs immortal new,
And tears will turn into morning dew !
Sorrow and joy but two sides of a coin,
Get up Melancholy and New year's merrymaking
join !

Life is the most precious gift,
You have ever received;
Don't waste it
As again you will never receive!

As New Year's Dawn breaks
Dark clouds of Covid will fade,
As 'farewell' to 'Dark-Year' you have bade,

Through 'clear waters' you will surely wade !
Satish Gaikwad December 27th 2020

16) Tarabai the Brave Maratha Queen

There at Satara
Rests in peace Queen Tara
The 'Rainha dos Maratha'
The 'shining star' of land of warrior
"Shambho,Mahadeo Har Har !"

In Talbid Village stood Maratha Warrior
Hambirrao Mohite Shivaji's Commander
'Tara'---shining star was his daughter
Astride horse, sword in hand Tara in war!

Aurangzeb the great Mughal Emperor,
Frustrated by Tara in great scare .
She kept Scarlet Flag flying high in Kolhapur
Brave Queen of long fought war rare !

Years passed by and the great, grand queen Tara,
Returned to her city Satara.
To live peaceful years in vicinity of fort
Ajinkyatara !
In nostalgia of victories in golden Era !

Tall stands Fort Ajinkyatara
Tall stands the Brevery of 'Ajinkya' 'Tara'
Glory of Maratha Kingdom and glory of Satara !

Rest in peace grand Queen 'Ajinkya'-'Tara' !
Satish Gaikwad December 26th 2020

Ajinkya = Invincible. Tara= Bright star
Tara is name of the queen
Har Har = Maratha Warrior's war slogan
'Ajinkyatara' name of fort meaning Invincible fort .
Portuguese addressed Tarabai as "Rainha dos
Maratha"

17) Covid19

But for Birth where would be the Death ?
Birth is the father of the Death !
When there is Sunrise, then only can there be
Sunset !
Life is story of one breath in and out one breath !

Life is journey of preset course !
Or is it journey governed by myself?
Can events in life I alter or shape ?
Then how can I or how much the Doctor can give
hope ?

Where from came the Vampire Bat ?
And set free the particles of virus from naught!
Corona kills millions of men,
And toil and struggle the Doctors in vain!

It's not for us humans
To kill men in war
The nature does it in his style ;
It's for us to nurse men meanwhile!

Every event has a lesson to learn
Does Covid not teach us when millions burn ?
What we need is love and coexistence,

Live and let me live in peace!

When one sneezes, Society gets Covid
Social responsibility is the key to prevent the
disease horrid .
Doctor will do what he does best
Social responsibility and duty must perform the
rest !

Nature will take Covid to its logical end
With horrible virus, God also immunity sends
Born virus has to die as birth brings death
Society living in harmony and peace... no one
can stop its breath!

Satish Gaikwad December 27th 2020

18) E=MC Sqare

From unknown dark,
I erupted in this world,
Like a seed sprouting out from soil .
And embarked on life journey of few miles!

Vast, boundless the Universe,
Short sighted me !
The sky is high,
No wings for me !

Know not me,
Where you are hidden.
Nor can I reach,
'Dark Horse' ridden!

When I close my eyes
Opens inner eye in well of mind
And one light bright
Ignites the mind with words kind
"Hark!" " Here am I " !

Gallops the 'Dark Horse' in speed of light,
And 'horse ridden' me turning into energy bright!

Expanding to bottomless Ocean with roar,
" E =Mc Square... E=Mc Square..E=Mc Square"!

Satish Gaikwad December 30eth 2020

19) Chipako

Farmers in the fields harvest reap,
Wandering Shepherds in meadows with happy
sheep
And Cedar trees on hill, company of clouds keep,
In a village on bank of river in Mountain
Himalaya!

Peace prevailed in the valley of mist,
Clear blue sky, snow crowned mountains kiss !
And lapping waters in the river, sing song
God knows one day what went wrong!

Axes in their hands, hacked the Cedar trees
unknown 'Savage men',
And shrubs and nettles they decimated then,
Turning the thick Forest into desert land,
Their appetite for land went on and on !

Villagers in tears, to the trees, they cling
Wailing and shouting, " Stop killing! Stop killing!"
;
Like loving children to their mothers cling !
And women and children form protecting ring !

'Chipako' their movement for 'Green Vision'

And the Parliament passed act on Forest
Conservation,
Merrily swing shrubs, nettles and Cedars Tall
As singing farmers answered the 'Nature's Call'

Satish Gaikwad January 1st 2021.

Chipako = To cling or hug
Chipako movement peaceful Gandhian method
resulted into Parliament passing Conservation Act
1980 .

20) Tai my sister

Tai .... my sister
Ever shining Star,
Or still better a lamp ..
Dim, burning in temple of Lord Krishna!

She imbibed hardships,
And turned into wax candle
Hard yet soft
To burn and turn into light !

She emits joy around
Wishing everyone well
Selfless to core
Shining and smiling ever !

In my journey of life
She is like standstill North Star
Or a lighthouse standing Tall,
And directing my canoe so far!
Satish Gaikwad January 2nd 2021

21) Dog's Life

When the night is dark,
And the soul takes its head out,
From the reef in the Ocean,
To hear the wailing sound !

The sound that tears apart,
The dead, frightful darkness to its core,
And shrill ripples spread on the night all over!
Including ripples over the sorrowful Ocean!

The dog howling, staring at the sky,
And questioning the unknown,
"Is it for suffering only you brought me here?"
"Or there is something more?"
" In my dog's life?"

" Every dog has his day,
The night will give way..
To bright dawn "
Answered the unknown!

"The morning Sun will shine through dew
Then you will be the one amongst a few

You are faithful, loving animal
Who will never sell his loyalty for his survival"

"Honesty and loyalty are your virtues best
Which make life worth living to your taste;
In misery, sheds tears even the king
But joyfully tail, only you can swing!" .

Satish Gaikwad January 6th 2021

22) Where is the Moon?

Where Is The Moon

Dark is the night
Stars are shining with smile wry
And silent is their cry
"Where is the Moon? "

Deep are the wounds
Bleeding is my heart
Numb pain smarts
"Where is the Moon?"

Night after night
Same story repeats
Now eyes are my dry
And silent is the cry
"Where is the Moon?"

When Jasmine fragrance the breeze wafts
And Crescent ☪ Moon sails soft
Then sweetly night croons

" Here is the Moon!"
"Here is the Moon !"

Satish Gaikwad January 10th 2021

23) Tailor Birds

Through windows of my living room hall,
I see dark green leaves of the decorative plants
Broad and long like Turmeric plannts'
Hidden from world outside by boundary wall .

One day, a pair of Tailor Birds small,
Spotted and selected the plant for their nest to be,
As security and safety was assured by the wall,
For their eggs and babies to be !

Beautiful birds, like small cotton balls
White feathers and grey shade overall
Needle like beaks and eyes twinkling stars
Alighted on the plant from the sky away sofar.

When on the wings the little birds would sing
And on the plant they would be merry making;
Artistically they sewed one leaf 🌿 with beak
The beak moved skillfully like a surgeon's Needle
quick 😄 !

So I thought more than Tailor Birds, Surgeons
were they,

Perfect suturing with beak's Needle and threads of
hay !
Thus they created most beautiful nest,
And pleased God, presented them pearl like two
eggs □an award Best !

Magically hatched the eggs, peeping two chicks
hungry
Wide open beaks, crying as if they were angry
Hurriedly brought some food the Bird-parents
And fed their hungry angry babies Godsent!

Some days later .. the babies got feather
And strength in their wings
And learned from parents how to sing
What a surprise one day they flew way with
skyward swing!

Stunned parents, were taken aback
Aggrieved they said looking at the nest
"Is this the way to depart best ?"
"Shouldn't they have spent more time in the nest?"

"Wish they would return to stay with us
Their company and love for us precious "
But that was not to happen ever
As they had left the nest for ever !

Satish Gaikwad January 9th 2021

24) Egret's Regret

In the Mangrove forest
I often see an Egret
Stalking in muddy water
Uplifted foot, softly landing in water.

Eyes fixed on the prey,
Gracefully slowly moves the neck
Such precise moves only this bird can make,
As forward moving leg one step takes!

Never makes sound a conch standstill !
Ever ready beak for prey to ensnare
Such a skill in bird very rare
Arrow like darts beak with fish in air !

When night spreads its veil dark
Fish sleep under water carefree
Whining the egret in nest on a tree
Too many fish he gobbled cause of his misery.
Repenting for fish killed too many

Colicky pain in stomach and retching
Sleepless, restless Egret in the nest tossing

" Can I not kill only few I need " said the Egret
" What is the sense in gobbling in greed and
regret ? "

Satish Gaikwad January 11th 2021

25) Anna- My Eldest Brother

'Anna' is my eldest brother,
His name is Prabhakar .
Means rising, soft Sun
My parent's first child - son .

' Graduate in every home ' oath my teacher-father
took from illiterate villagers one 'dark night'.
An early graduate Anna showed the light .
He proved his name right and lived up to his
father's dream
He became professor and enlightened so many of
them

Remained soft and simple Prabhakar -
The Sun bringing dawn of education for farmers ;

He didn't change with time as no watch ever on his
wrist,
He treaded path of life as teacher to meet his father
at the 'illuminated village' their Tryst !

Satish Gaikwad January 15th 2021

26) Mother Please Forgive ME

Mother you brought me in this beautiful world,
In your song I heard the first word .
When Cuckoo started to sing
And in swinging flowers danced the Spring!

Your hand had magical touch turning pain
into pleasure,
You caressed my cheeks the breeze did it to
backyard flowery treasure,
Through your eyes I peered the meadows green,
And your ears made me listener to bleating lambs,
keen !

Mother you were my Doctor and love was your
medicine,
When I became your Doctor, I always remained
your son, keen,
Patience, sympathy, empathy and so many things,
You taught me, till you left for heaven on your wings!

Memories are sweet ; memories do kill
What's lasting for ever, is your strong will
'To love, to forgive, and to live and let live '
Mother, if I fall short please forgive!

Satish Gaikwad January 14th 2021

27) No Shadow of War

I thought the path I treaded
Is coming to the end and in obscurity
I will lie at your feet dumb,
In peace with all senses numb!

The hatred, jealousy, anger and prejudice,
All will leave me alone,
And air that I will breathe filled in with your
music,
And your symphony will mingle with my moan !

My legs are free from fetters but I will not trudge,
As I prefer to lie in clover at your feet with
pleasure huge !
Peaceful will be the nights and the sky full of stars

And bright will be the days with no
 shadows of wars !

Satish Gaikwad January 17th 2021

28) Conceited 'Brainy Animal'

Mighty Nature! His hour clock has second hand
Running with speed of hundreds years a second
And games he plays of 'evolution' with magical
thought
Turning monkeys to men and dinosaurs □
to naught!

In his magic show, he made monkey 🐒 to stand up
right
Called him 'man' and gave him 'future' bright !
Thousands of 'silicon chips ' he put in man's brain
□
And asked him to take the Earth's reign!

With thousands of 'silicon chips' in, swollen his
head
"Now I will decide " Conceited man

boastfully said !
"Who lives and how!" "Nature is for me and l am
not for him "
And killed animals, birds and trees so many of
them!

He asserted " animals and trees ⚥ are for my need"
The nature provided to his needs but not to his greed--
'Killing for pleasure and wars for fun'
Recklessly intoxicated man went on run !

Nature's clock ticked 'Ringing Alarm ' ☐
Shaking the Earth with its 'mighty arm
Tremors felt all over such was the 'Earthquake '
Boastful man over looking warning said " Oh! I don't shake "

'How small you are, I will let you know '
Said the Nature and sent invisible Corona

To remind ' Dinosaurs ☐ were brought to naught '
'Brainy Animal ' give it some thought!

Satish Gaikwad January 19th 2021

29) My Torn Soul

The Sun hides himself behind the mountain range
As the golden hue dying soft in the sky ,
Seagulls and cormorants loudly cry ,
And walks in stealthily, the night with smile wry .

The world of nocturnals awakes joyfully
And dogs, foxes, hyenas come out slowly,
Under diamond studded sky, their stary night
festival
Sometimes my soul joins them in such a carnival .

As I was lying on bed, on one such night
Eyes closed, mind awake with weird thoughts,
I heard hyena laughing his lung out,

And in the Mangrove forest was there a silence
fraught!

A group of dogs was merry making nearby
In wailful choir they suddenly started to cry !
Laughing hyena and wailing- dogs mourn
And between these two was my soul torn.

'Hoot, Hoot,Hoot!' said the Owl
"Death of prey is the killer's joy ..
Much unnecessary your helpless cry
Relax! Time to heal your torn soul "
Thus said the wise Owl !

Satish Gaikwad January 22nd 2021

30) Mother's Hand

In dark starry night
When world around me sleeps
In serene silence I leisurely peep
Into storehouse of mind in memories sweet!

In month of August, holding mother's hand
I walk through flowering plants on rocky land,
In blue, yellow flowers, Bulbuls and Wrens call
Besides lapping waters of Akaladevi Brook
waterfall

Shravan's songs on mother's lips
And dancing me on my toe tips;
Bleating lambs on Sunny hilly bourn
And twittering quails run in a field of corn !

Such are the memories of morning vibes
With golden rays in sky the Sun scribes,
As smile the flowers on rocky land
I feel the warmth of the mother's hand !

Satish Gaikwad January 25th 2021

31) Statues

Haggard, wretched, tramp searching space in
Megacity,
Thirsty, hungry he moves around, ...what a pity !
Could not spot land even one Sqare foot
To sit or at least rest his foot !

On acres and acres of beautiful land
On high pedestal proudly they stand
Majestic statues of men dead,
' Let me rest here' the wretched tramp said!

' Get lost from here ' the crowd there said
'Celebrating his Birthday today ' pointing at
statue's head
Said Statue worshipers there in anger
And tears dropped from the tramp's eyes
as he moved away in hunger !

Statues in abundance every corner and nook
Appreciating the gardens around them in 'deadly'
look !
In happiness and peace live the 'Statues of Men '
dead
While hungry, haggard tramp lives half dead!

Satish Gaikwad January 27th 2021

(Translation of Marathi poem from
my poetry book 'Gahivaralele Zendu)

32) Paper Boat

Half a verse I scribed on a paper
Struggled invain to give it a name proper
Now, even the paper is not traceable
And rewriting that verse impossible !

"What are you searching Daddy?" "Is it the
paper?"
"Oh ! I made a paper boat of it " said my daughter.
"Look at the lake, how beautifully does it sail."
"Doesn't it look like running cute quail ? "

Peering at the lake, I wondered, 'who will
appreciate now my 'verse innominate'
Fish or Tortoises can't even read it '
'If the paper boat sinks in its lake - sojourn
Would those words to me ever return?'

At the far end of the lake
I spotted the boat as a white speck
Swirled for few minutes before it sank
Along with 'innominate verse ' in lake blank.

Felt I like a mother who had missed abortion,
The half verse, as if it was my body portion

Agonies of unborn child gone
With pains and moans life went on !
(Few months later.....)

As I was looking at the lake one full moon night
Bewitching Moon and shining light
Words I heard intoning soft
Echoes of lines of my verse in the lake lost.

"Innominate we arrive from naught
Who gives us name,boat and beautiful thoughts ?
Droning we do sing, but 'half the Verse'
Before we sink in the 'boundless Universe'!"

Satish Gaikwad January 30th 2021

(Translated poem from my Marathi poem book
Shevantichya Pakalya)

33) Wonderland of Nostalgia

When weather becomes cool in June rainfall,
Distant cooing wood pigeon calls,
And mind takes to wings to travel in past
Into 'wonderland of nostalgia' vast

July brings torrential rain
Dim lamp struggles to illuminate home in vain :
My mother baking roties on earthen hearth
Dark home brightens with her heart's warmth!

As I stand on bank of pond frogs in water joyfully
swim
Croaking they call their mates to fulfill their
'family dream'!
Floating leaves in water, white Lillies dance,

And spreading glassy wings Dragonflies glance !

Branch of mango tree happily swings
As Cuckoo perching on it sweetly sings
Green Jowar plants nod on the rhythm of the song
And shepherd plays flute at distance long !

Such are bygone days' charms
Love, warmth and shelter in mother's arms
When you take journey to past,
Into 'wonderland of nostalgia '-vast !

Satish Gaikwad February 2nd 2021

Transalated from my poetry book 'Shevantichya
Pakalya'

34) Come to Us with your mighty sword

When fleecy clouds conceal stars
And friends engage in shadow wars
I remember you the savior my Lord
Come to us with your mighty sword !

When untruth and violence becomes order of the
day
Honesty, hard work and trust run away
Boundless ocean of humanity turns coward
Come to us with your mighty sword

When shining tower of riches skywards grows
And hungry, naked labourers get crushed under
their toes
And rulers forget the Father of Nation's words
My Lord Come to us with your mighty sword !

Satish Gaikwad February 3rd 2021

35) Doctor Me

Serving humans is my mission
Doctor ! Me by profession !
Day, dark night or lovely dawn,
My work just goes on...!

Elders fall ! Like winter-fall leaves
To them I say " Bye 🖐 Goodbye!"
But when blooming-bud leaves
Helplessly I ask " Why? Why ? "

My war against Death, endless though,
Many battles won and many I lost ;
Life never caeses but continues to flow!
Seeds sprout in burial-land, as melts frost!

Such is my commitment to profession
Caring for every soul with passion
Tied to the profession by stethoscope around neck
Fight with death will continue, whatever it takes!

Satish Gaikwad February 9th 2021
(Translated poem from my Marathi poetry
Book Shevantichya Pakalya)

36) Freedom to Fly

When I walk through narrow lonely gorge
Bubbling waters and rocks around large
Where blinding vision, veil of mist looms large
On timid mind like scary animal savage !

Suffocated soul, longing for sky
Begging for wings and freedom to fly
In boundryless world and clear skies
Free from passport and visas... timid mind cries!

Where birds sing in sweet symphony
And barriers of languages melt into language of
heart like honey
Ponds of castes and creed merge to be boundless
Ocean
And humanity spreads out its wings of love and
passion!

There the world is ruled by God's laws
Buried underground all human flaws
There the clouds can't hide shining stars
Peaceful nights and far away wars !

Satish Gaikwad February 13th 2021

37)On that Day in the Month of June

Dark clouds gathered in the sky
Secrets in heart and tears in their welled up eyes,
They crouched down on the hill, about to cry
On that day in the month June .

While leaving for the office I said "Bye"
To my mother who looked into my eyes
'Ocean of love ' in her eyes !
With love, her gaze filled my heart soon
On that day in the month of June

Her eyes spoke in language of heart
Conveying to me what millions of words can not
Story of my own life- 'a bud blooming from her
womb to a busy doctor zooming '
On that day in the month of June.

Smile on her face with shade of sadness
trace
Secrets of angina she held in her heart
Her eyes told me story of her life
'Love, endurance and and pangs of angina rife '
On that day in the month of June.

In afternoon, I received call from my wife
'Mother sinking and agonizing angina pain'
I rushed to the site and struggled to save her life
With all skill at command of a doctor... struggle in
vain
On that day in the month of June

"I am fine" "you take care "
Said she hiding angina pain unbearable
Those soulful eyes, 'Ocean of love'
Were bidding Goodbye to her doctor-son
miserable.
On that day in the month of June

I saw my mother struggling for breath
Her water flooded lungs and angina torn heart
And 'Iron hand' of dreadful Death!
'Love Ocean ' dried up in dead glassy eyes
And the Sun hid behind dark clouds in gloomy sky
Torrential downpour of heavenly
tears in afternoon
On that day in the month of June

Satish Gaikwad March 5th 2021

38) Since Long

Since long......
I long to go to my village
There in clear water of Akaladevi Brook minows
swim leisurely
On the bank goats nonchalantly ruminate cud
As merrily dance snipes in the mud
And lightly humming birds kiss blooming-buds

There peace spreads its wings as veil of mist
And happily shepherds wander in wilderness
With sheep flock moving from place to place
And shining Sun in the sky their witness

Thirsty sheep run to the Brook in afternoon
Bells ring, swinging freely around their neck
Each bell, though rings with different tune,
Together symphony sweet they do make
There on the bank of the Brook in afternoon

I long to go there and lie down under stary sky
Where wailful crickets mournfully cry
And I will listen to their sad stories and songs
As Crescent Moon asks them 'what went wrong?'

Satish Gaikwad March 9th 2021

39) Green Bee Eater

On the telephone wires
Parallel to railway lines
For few minutes sits a Green Bee Eater
And darts suddenly later
In air to catch insects flying

The villagers call it 'Mad Parrot'
Who swings on telephone wires
Counting trains passing by
And merrily dances in air when it flies
To catch the gay butterflies
Displaying its green wings the bird slye

There is method in its madness
Swinging on the wires and counting trains
While aiming at bees and butterflies careless
And dancing in air on the catch the bird merciless!

Satish Gaikwad March 24th 2021

The Green Bee Eater is called 'Veda Raghu '
in Marathi language meaning 'Mad Parrot'

40) My Grandson Vivaan

Life is beautiful 😊
Is it because there are stars
Flowers smile and birds sing around

Or is it due to lambs 🐑 bleating sound ?

May that be so .....
Joy abundant I gather

From all of them put together 🖤
Yet the pleasure is nowhere
Nearer to the joy and care
My grandson Vivaan provides to me
When he says "Nana!" and dances

His face lit up with impish glee 😬 !

Satish Gaikwad March 25th 2021

41)I am but their part

I have come to this world to love 💘
Blooming buds and singing birds 🐦
To listen to ecstatic Cuckoo or pensive cooing
Dove ☐
And translate their joy or anguish into my words .

The Sparrows in my yard merrily dance
Hidden Owl ☐ in burrow I spot by chance
Hurriedly running Lizards I see in scurry
I do feel and understand their great worry!

In dewdrops shines morning golden Sun
Hidden seeds sprout in soil, .. such a great fun
In crystal clear tears melts my heart ♥
On realizing I am but their integral part !

Satish Gaikwad March 28th 2021

42) Surendra

He was truly like bright  Sun
Who restricted himself to his dark study
Million Rays shining his notebook lines
And the world outside thought of him

'Clouded sky dim Moon ☽

But he was Su(n)-Ray-(I)ndra --- The ☀

****

My Brother Surendra passed away on 26th April 2021

43) Mystical Star

Distant shining Star - Thee
Thousands of light years away from me,
Still closer to my heart ♥
Nearest and dearest thou art !

Incomprehensible thy relation to me
Inaccessible thy throne!
Enthralling thy charm, sets me free
To soar heavenwards to meet Thee .

Dark is the Universe
Darker is my heart ♥
Single ray of hope traverses
While brightly shining thou art .

The hope you raise in night
Instantly dies in day's light ;
Why do you ignite in me passion?
Mortal destined me to sink in Ocean.

Sore is my heart today, why do you blink ?
Tell me in clear words before I sink;
What is the message in language of ray □
What do you convey from so far away?

****

Mystical Star ✮, bewitching her smile
Wordless though she was,
Something she did tell me worthwhile
Dear she thought of me because.

In language of rays wordless though
Said she "I love 💝 you "-
Message through rays that made you sore
Sent by me thousands of years before "

"Ceaseless and restless I searched for you
For thousands of years through messenger Ray
Where were you and in what form ? Hey !
Hide and seek you changed your forms
While faithful me adhered to norms ".

"Hide and seek' is your game
'Eternity and love' is my name 💓,
You change your form time and again
My love for you remains the same "

"I will continue to shine
As rays are language of mine
You alone will translate it in verse
While love traverses the Universe!"

Satish Gaikwad

(Translated poem from my Marathi poetry Book
Shevantichya Pakalya)

67

44) Universal Soul

Myopics are we by birth,
Shallow is our vision
Bodies we do see on the Earth,
Forgetting the souls deep within!

Birds, animals are but eatables for us,
Do we really live upto our conscience?
The souls in them are as precious,
As much as we think of us .

How can we forget from one unicellular organism
We all evolved the kingdom of animals
Thus we are bound, our soul Universal
It's on you 'Brainy Animal' to care for the
'Soul Universal '
Satish Gaikwad January 26th 2021

45) Maestro Thou Art

Oh ! My Lord .....
How Beautiful is thy creation !
Thy minstrels tirelessly sing,
In praise of Thee, yet the songs are not over,
The birds, bees and brooks sing for ever!

The greatest Maestro thou art
Your orchestra creates finest of the Art !
When I lie in solitude....
In air thou fillest the music sweet!
And in the sky in harmony the birds tweet!

Sweetly singing Cuckoo welcomes the Spring,
And for Autumn's harvest the Megapie sings !
Summer's songs in the Bulbul's sound
And sweet your melody year around!

Love is your language .....
And melodious symphony you arrange
For the life to sing in your tune,
When in serene silence sings full Moon!

Satish Gaikwad January 3rd 2021

About the Author

Dr Satish Gaikwad

He completed his MBBS and MD in General Medicine from G. S. Medical College and KEM Hospital Mumbai and served as Director Medical Services of

Air India. Presently he is Consultant Physician.

He has keen interest in science and the Nature. He published two poetry books in Marathi language. He was the first person

to introduce in Marathi literature the concept of poetry arises from the core of

science. He wrote poems on Darwin's theory, Einstein theory and so many others

He received N. C. Kelkar Award for his autobiography 'Smriti Pakhare'

'Chrysanthemom' is his first English poetry book .

www.ingramcontent.com/pod-product-compliance
Lightning Source LLC
Chambersburg PA
CBHW052220150726
48002CB00003B/1197